Read me a Story

Tales to Share

hinkler

Published by Hinkler Books Pty Ltd
45–55 Fairchild Street
Heatherton Victoria 3202 Australia
www.hinkler.com.au

hinkler

Cover Illustration: Laura Watkins
Prepress: Graphic Print Group

ISBN: 978 1 7436 3544 5

Printed and bound in China

Contents

It's not JUST a blanket!

Written and illustrated by
ANNALIESE STONEY

For Steve and my family, for all their cheerleading!

It's not
JUST
a blanket...

Sophia *loved* her blanket **VERY** much.

Everywhere...

and ANYWHERE

that she and her dog Monty went,

the blanket came too!

Her family didn't understand why.

"It's **JUST** a blanket!"

they said.

But Sophia knew better.

"It's <u>not</u> **JUST** a blanket. It's a..."

11

MUNCH MUNCH

It's not JUST a blanket!
It's a...

Slippery stingray!

It's not JUST a blanket! It's a...

PIRATE SHIP!

It's not **JUST** a blanket!
Look! It's a...

17

And it's not JUST a blanket! It's a...

And it's not **JUST** a blanket! It's a...

21

SNOOZING

BAT!

In fact, because it's not JUST a blanket, it's worth...

27

Poor Sophia was very upset.

Monty felt pretty bad, too.

Her brother Clive saw the whole thing.

He told the whole family,

who thought very hard, until eventually they came up with

A BRILLIANT PLAN...

$mc^2 = \frac{1}{4}$

First, Dad collected all the torn bits of blanket.

Clive took off his starry socks.

Grandma found an old pair of bloomers,

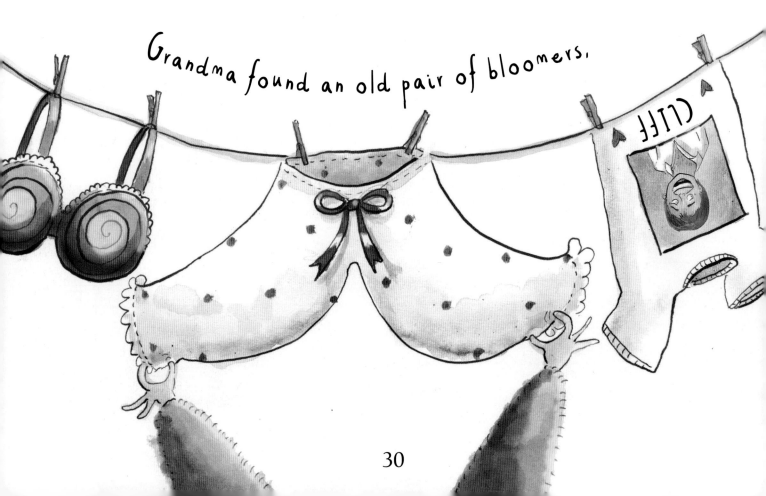

and Mum generously donated Dad's Hawaiian shirt collection.

Then, armed with a big bundle of material, they worked very, very hard, until...

"TA-DA!" they exclaimed.
"Here you are Sophia and Monty. We know how much you loved that old blanket, so we've made you BOTH new blankets."

"Thank you very much!" Sophia and Monty said.

"The only thing is...

"They're

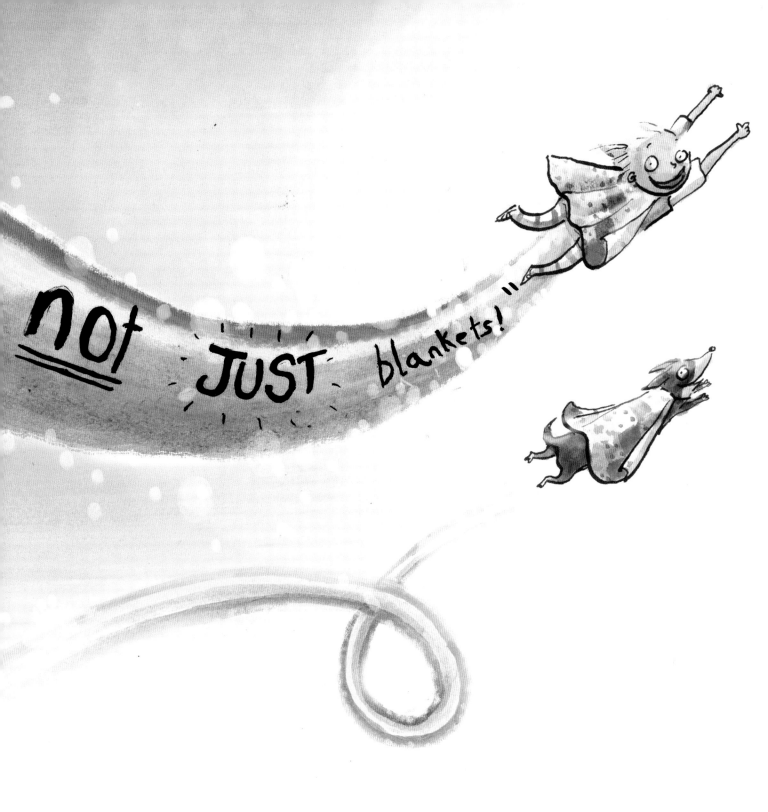

To my son Eric

Chomp

Written by Melissa Mattox
Illustrated by Mark Chambers

Today was Chomp's first day at school. He was afraid he wouldn't make any new friends. He swam slowly behind his dad towards the coral gates of the school as the other fish darted and splashed out of their way.

"Keep your dorsal fin up and don't forget to smile," said Chomp's dad reassuringly.

Chomp nodded, but he could hear whispers from a passing pod of dolphins. "I hope I'm not in the shark's class," said one.

"There's no way anyone is going to want to sit next to him," hissed another.

Chomp tried to remember what his dad said about smiling, but he knew it wouldn't be easy.

It seemed that everyone already had lots of friends.

43

Chomp tried to introduce himself to his fellow classmates. He remembered what his father said and did his best smile.

"Hello, I'm..."

...but nobody wanted to talk to him.

At the playground, things didn't get much better.

Chomp tried to join in with hide and seek.

"...nine, ten. I'm coming to get you!"

...but nobody wanted to play.

Everywhere he went, Chomp felt like he didn't belong.

When lunchtime came, Chomp still hadn't made one single friend.

He collected his lunch but noticed something was missing. He swam over to a nearby table.

"**AHHHH!** Please don't eat us!" screamed the crab.

AHHHH!

"Eat you? I would never eat you!" laughed Chomp.

"I'm a vegetarian! Could you possibly pass the sea salt please?"

After that, the other fish found they had a lot more in common with Chomp than they'd thought.

From then on, things seemed
to go much easier!

Chomp and his class went to
visit historical sites.

They practised their
fishing-line knots.

And they even played Chomp's
favourite game of 'chase'!

To Rowan - MM

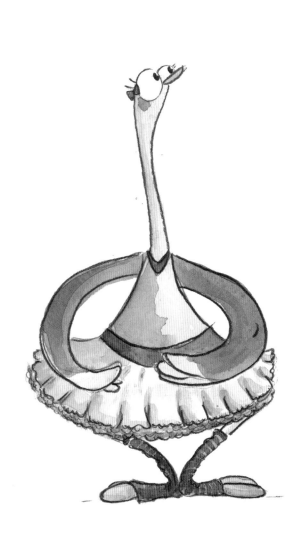

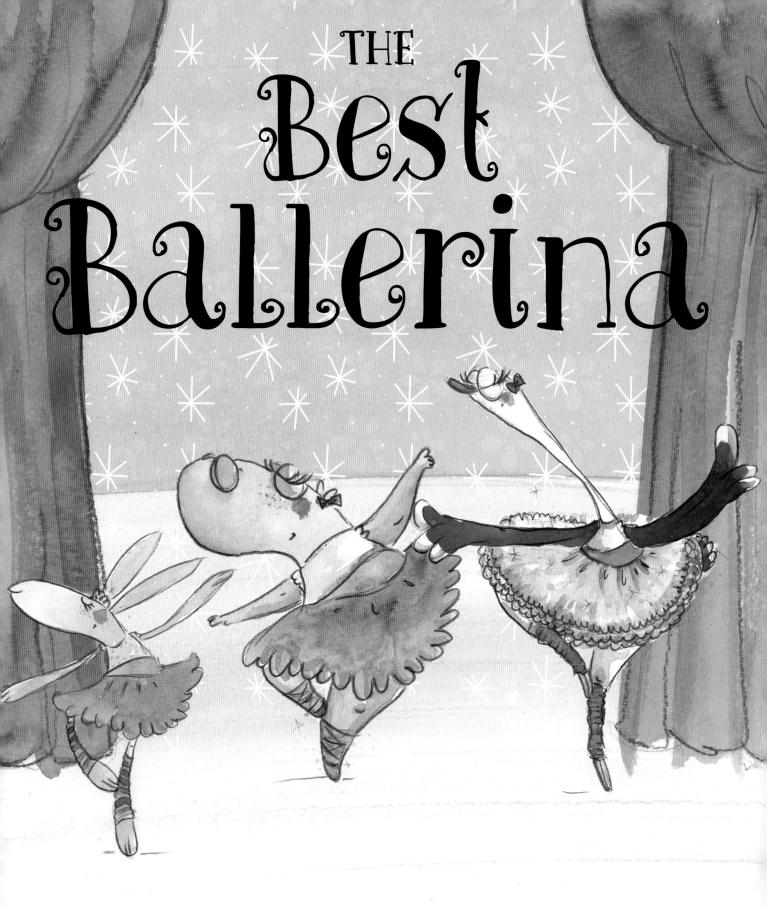

THE Best Ballerina

Melissa Mattox   Irisz Agócs

By the end of the day, Chomp had made so many friends that by the time his dad showed up, he didn't want to leave.

"Please, can I stay here?" he begged. Chomp's dad laughed.

"Don't worry," said Miss Blowfish. "Tomorrow's lesson is something you can really sink your teeth into."

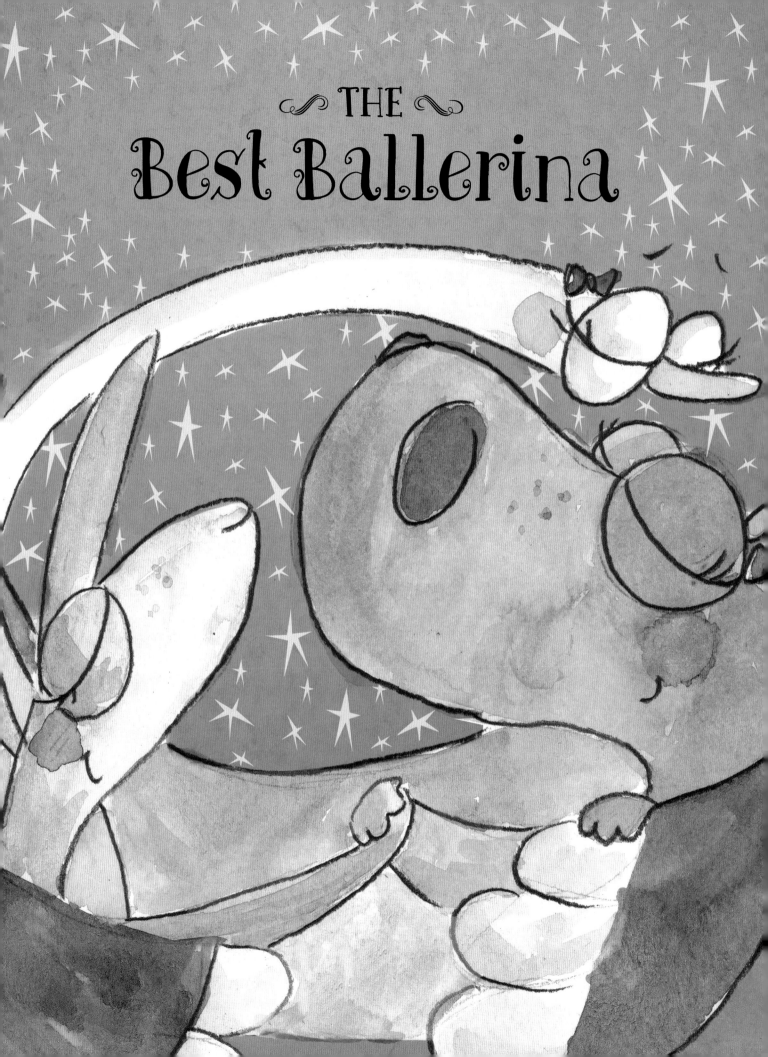

THE
Best Ballerina

Harriet was so excited. She wanted to show her
friends her new ballet slippers.

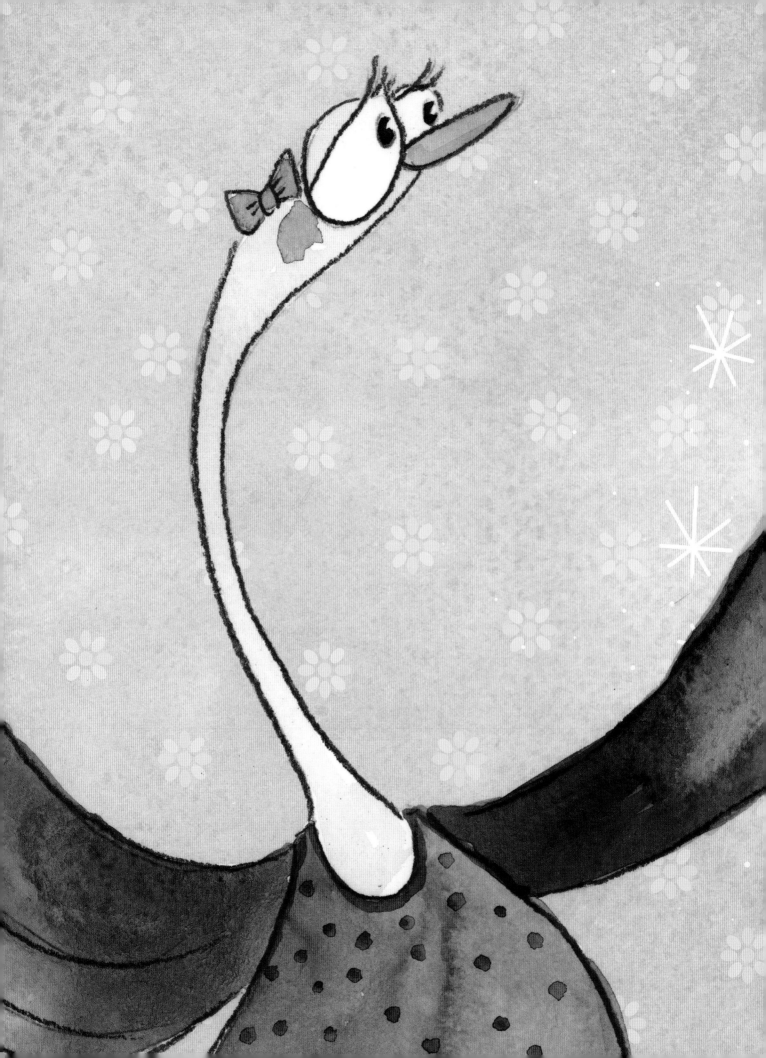

"Those are beautiful! And they match my tutu perfectly," said Olivia. "Together they will make a perfect fairy-princess costume."

"Not without this, they don't!" said Rachel.

"Ooooh," hummed the girls, happily.

The three friends twirled and spun, leaped and pirouetted.

As they danced, all they could think about was the upcoming big ballet recital.

"Oh no! I just realised something," said Harriet, stopping mid-dance. "We only have enough pieces for one fairy-princess costume.

Only one of us can dance in the big ballet recital!"

"Well, it should be me," said Olivia.
"I have the longest legs."

"But I brought the tiara!" interrupted Rachel.

"That shouldn't matter!"
cried Harriet.

Each girl tried on the costume.

But no matter how hard they tried, it just didn't look right.

The friends continued to argue, each one convinced that she was the best fairy-princess dancer.

"Ladies, why all the fussing?" asked Madam Hoot.

Harriet, Olivia, and Rachel explained the problem.

Madam Hoot listened carefully.

"The night sky is never lit by just one star but shines because there are many," she said. "Why don't you three get some rest? Tomorrow you can choose who should wear the costume at the recital."

That night the girls lay in their beds, staring up at the dark night sky, all lit up with hundreds of twinkling starry lights.

The next morning, the three friends met before the dance.

89

"I'm sorry we fought," said Rachel. "I think Harriet should dance. She has the best twirls."

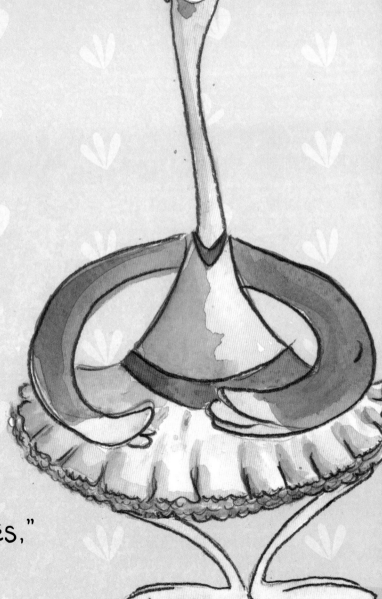

"But Olivia has the best pliés," said Harriet.

"No one can beat Rachel's leaps,"
offered Olivia.

92

A crowd had gathered to watch the girls perform.
"Bravo!" "Hooray!" "Magnificent!" they shouted.

"I think the best fairy princess for the big ballet recital should be ... all three of us!" said Olivia. "Together we make true fairy-princess magic!"

To my son Eric – MM
To lovely Sam, welcome to the family – MT

The Great TORTOISE & HARE Counting Race

3

2

1

12

11

10

MELISSA MATTOX • MICHAEL TERRY

"I'm counting," says Tortoise.

"Counting? I **love** to count!"

"Me too! Now, please don't interrupt," says Tortoise. "**4, 5, 6**..."

"**7, 8, 9**!" Hare shouts, bouncing up and down. "And... wait, what comes after **9**?"

"**10**," says Tortoise, "but don't count so fast."

But Hare doesn't listen.

"11, 12, 13, 14..." giggles Hare.

"Wait!" Tortoise shouts.

"**15, 16** ..." says Hare.

"Be patient," says Tortoise.
"I'm getting there."

"*Tortoise*!
What comes after **16**?"

"I must know!" sobs Hare.
"The suspense is **unbearable**!"

"This wait is exhausting!
I think I'll take a nap."

1 2 3 4 5

6 7 8 9 10 11 12 13

"Oh no, I overslept!" Hare wails. "Wait, what's this?"

"**17**! How could I forget you **17**? I love you **17, 18, 19**..."

"**20**," Tortoise says.

"I knew that," says Hare.

"Now, let's count backwards! **20**, **19**, **18**, **17**, **16**..."

126

"Hold on, I'm coming!" says Tortoise. "**15, 14, 13, 12...**"

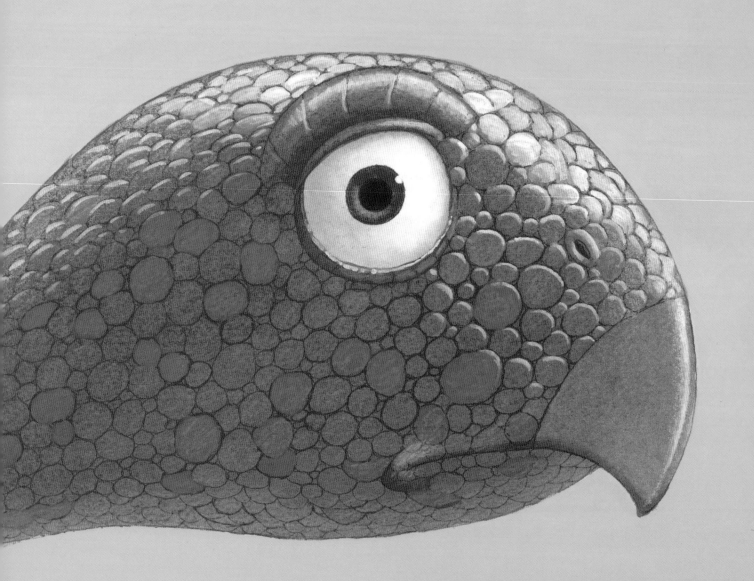

For my sister Rosie

Rosie's room

Lucy **loved** horses.

Not just a little...

...but a **lot**!

She had a
horse bike,

she had a horse bag,

she had  horse slippers,

 but she didn't have a **horse**.

"Muuuuuuuuuuuum…" Lucy begged. "Please, please, please can I have a horse for my birthday?"

"Let's wait and see!" said Mum.

The morning of her birthday, Lucy raced downstairs
to find a big pile of presents.
"None of these look like a horse," she thought.

142

"We have one last present for you," said Dad, "but you have to close your eyes!"

Lucy closed her eyes as tightly as she could...

"SURPRISE!"

"What is **THAT**!?" Lucy asked.
"It's a pony!" said Mum. "Don't you like him?
His name is Hamish."

"**THAT** is not a real horse," Lucy sulked.

Lucy didn't love Hamish,

but Hamish loved Lucy.

She tried to ignore him,

but he followed her everywhere.

The next day was Lucy's birthday party.

"We have one last surprise for you," said Mum.

It was a ride on a very **big**, very **tall** horse.

"I HATE HORSES! They're too big!" screamed Lucy.

Now, Lucy **loves** Hamish!

clip clop clip clop

Love

Helen O'Dare

Nicola O'Byrne

This book is for all the special people in my life,
and especially for the most special of all, Reay and Bridie – HO'D

Love

can be **gigantic** like a **mountain**,
and **small** and **precious** like a **diamond**.

Love

stretches up, up, **tall** like a **tree**,
but secured by its **roots** so **deep**.

168

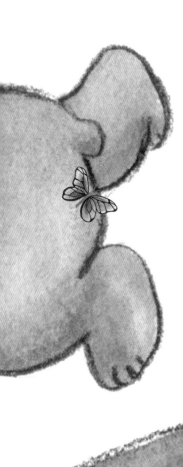

Love

has **wings** that help you **fly**
above the **clouds** in the **big blue sky**.

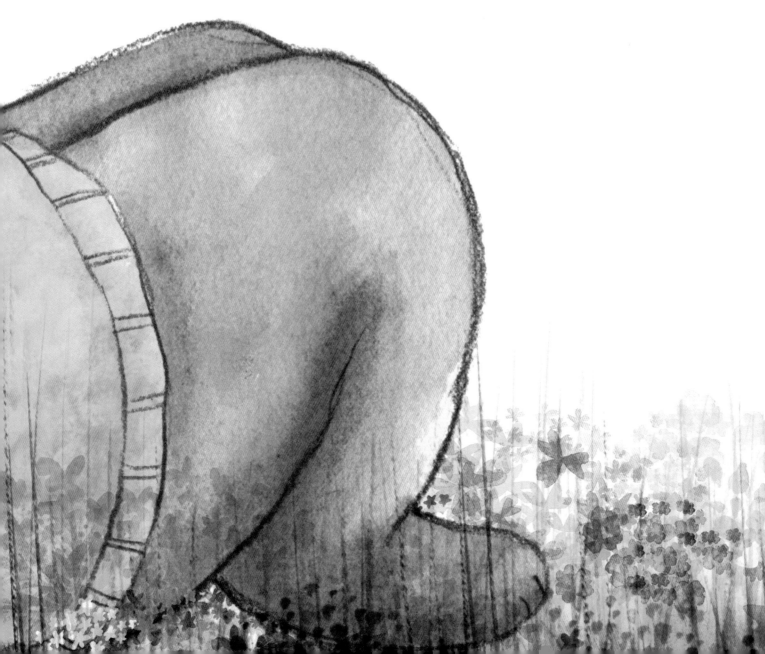

Love

is there in a **tickle** and a **giggle**
and an **enormous** belly-laugh **wiggle!**

can be **loud** like a trumpet's **blares**
that sometimes **catch** you **unawares**!

Love

is a **book** and a **warm** milk mug,
and makes the **rainy** days all **snug**.

Love

can be **yummy,**
like a **chocolate cake**
that we mixed and put
in the **oven** to **bake.**

Love

can make you **sing** out **loud**.
You always make me feel so **proud**!

Love

can be **splashes** and **soap** and **bubbles**.
I will always **love** your **cuddles**!

Love

is **strong** and **true** like a **big bear hug**
that you give to a **sleepy** little **snuggle-bug**.

Love
is **big** and **wide**
and **ocean deep**.
It's even **there**
when you're **asleep**.

Love
is all of these, it's true.
And that's how much
I love YOU!

189